A Crowded Mind

By

JB Baretsky

To my Grandfather, who lived and continues to live the great American life, and who has inspired me everyday of my life.

Thank you, Pop.

The Provider : War Time

Buried somewhere in the back of my closet is a piece of paper, a paper that states many things. It's a paper that says I served in the United States Marine Corps from 1946 to 1948. It says that I was a sharp shooter, a Military Police officer, and that I was honorably discharged. On the back, on one of the last lines, it also says that I was awarded the World War II victory medal. I'm writing this to help you understand why I will never wear that medal for as long as I live.

You see, I never touched the beaches at Normandy, I never felt the icy grip of Bastogne, and I never trekked through the mud at Iwo Jima. I instead served my country on the pristine white shores of Puerto Rico. It was a paradise, far from the horrors and brutalities of the Nazi and the Japanese armies. Who was I to be spared from all that? Just some skinny kid from the Catskills who wanted to get out of his little town and find some adventure. I had grown up running in the streets, eating tar from the freshly poured roads, telling the latest jokes to my friends and classmates, and putting on shows wherever I could. When we were flying into the sir strip there, I remember thinking that just a few months ago I was juggling rubber balls in the senior class talent skit, and now here I was, a real marine in freshly pressed khakis with a gun.

Speaking of guns, I want to go on record and say that the .45 they issued as my sidearm was the most inaccurate weapon I ever held. It's a bit of a random thought but, the only way to hit a target was to throw the actual gun at someone rather than pulling the trigger. I never thought I was much of a shot anyway, but I'm sure the pistol was to blame. During the end of my time there, I was assigned to the security detail for the President when he visited the Island. There I was, my .45 on my hip, and all I kept thinking was,

"Oh God I hope I don't have to shoot anyone." How embarrassing it would have been to miss a, would be, presidential assassin.

Anyway, I was given a great little job checking out and logging in athletic equipment for the base. I had my little desk, with a clipboard and a pen, and as someone borrowed a glove or a ball, I checked it off the list. At the end of the day, I counted to make sure we had the same number of balls, gloves, etc., as we had started with. It wasn't difficult obviously, and it wasn't an adventure, but it let me be around the unit when they were just being guys, not soldiers. That's a big deal. All the other time it was marching, training, shooting.

Once during basic in Parris Island, we went marching. If Puerto Rico was a paradise, Parris Island was hell. Apart from the usual rude awakening of military introductions, I was put into a gas chamber with nothing but an old mask from the first world war, and I saw a young enlistee, upon laughing while we were supposed to be at attention, asked to sit on a fire hydrant bareass until it was inside of him. Yea, what's that saying about not being in Kansas anymore? Well I've never been to Kansas but I'm sure as hell that shit wasn't happening there.

Now when we marched we did so for what seemed like an endless amount of time, and this particular day, when I had had enough of it, I turned to the back of the formation, and eyed this truck following closely behind us. I figured, I'd make like I was passing out and they'd throw me in the back of the flatbed. Now, no sooner did I have that bright idea, did the guy next to me drop like a sack of shit. I mean this kid looked dead. The whole troop stopped as the Sergeant made his way to the body bound in soaked khaki and checked his wrist. After waiting a few seconds he said something I never forgot,

"Leave him," he bellowed.
We all stared in amazement,

"I said leave him! Move! Double time lets go!"
And away we went. The poor bastard came crawling back to the barracks dragging his rifle at two in the morning. So yea, sports equipment was a nice break from the serious business.

My job though, wasn't serious. It was handing out baseballs and basketballs, laughing it up with the guys. It was where I really started making friends, it was there that I started lifting weights. I did overhead press,military press they call it now, it's an awful thing. I can still feel the pain sticking in the lower part of my back even now. I was always meant to be a skinny kid I guess. It was near the weights that I first met Kiershbaum. When you think of an image of what a United States Marine was supposed to be, it was him. This guy had triceps like steaks, shoulders like a moose. I first saw him hanging upside down doing sit ups, with a fifty pound plate behind his head. I remember asking him,

"So you gonna shoot the Japs? Or just rip them in half?"

He laughed, thank god.

That was it, we were buddies from that point on. He'd always make sure to introduce me to all the new guys when I came around. He knew everybody, probably because everybody wanted to know him, he even knew the guys that were coming back from overseas. He'd tell me who they were, where they'd been, what'd they'd seen, and all I had to offer these guys were a few stories, a few jokes, and a smile. Then I'd be on my way, hearing the laughter behind me as I left.

One morning, Kiershbaum was having a catch with a guy named Ryan, and the ball sailed over his glove and ended up right at my feet. Not thinking much of it, I picked it up and fired back in their direction,

"Hey Ski!"

That's what everyone called me, that's what they called anyone with a slovic sounding name,

"You want a spot on the team?"

Not wanting to disappoint the big guy I yelled back,

"Sure!"

"What position do you play?"

I thought for a second,

"What position do you need?"

Kiershbaum threw his head back in laughter,

"We don't got a pitcher!"

"Well you're in luck," I quipped, "I'm a pitcher." That's how I became the pitcher for the Marine Corps team for two years.

I never played organized ball before. I used to play with the kids in Hudson, in the cinder lots on the banks of the river. We had about four gloves and two bats between all of us and we'd all come home covered in dirt and soot only to wash, sleep and do it all over the next day. Now I was on an actual team, and was given a pair of cleats. I never wore cleats before in my life. I took one step and nearly fell over. I couldn't walk in the damn things. I ended up playing every game in my boots. I never figured out why that was. I can only relate it to when I was eight years old, and I got my ankles run over by a delivery truck. I noticed years later that because of that accident I couldn't ice or roller skate. Maybe it's why I couldn't walk in a pair of cleats. At least that's a better explanation than just being a spastic.

I don't remember much of the specifics of the games, probably because we weren't very good. I do remember having a bunch of fun though, always jawing and yammering with my teammates and the other teams. The other teams we played had a lot of guys who had seen action, real action, real shit. These were guys that had trouble sleeping at night, so how could I not shake their hand and try to get a smile out of them?

There was one particular afternoon that always sticks out when I think of those days on the ball field. We were practicing, trying to figure out how to win a game and this jeep rolled up, and out stepped this Sergeant Major. He started saying hello and shaking hands with everyone when someone asked him if he had ever played any ball. He said he had a little, so of course I started walking out to the rubber to throw him a few.

As I sauntered my way to the mound, I caught a quick glimpse of the officer taking off his jacket,

" He's bigger than I thought," I whispered to myself. I started rubbing up the ball when suddenly Kiershbaum screamed from the dugout,

"Throw it by him, Ski!"

"I'll make it quick!" I hollered back.

That was of course all bullshit because I never had much of a fastball. I did however, have the ability to place the ball damn near anyplace I wanted. I gazed to my catcher to get the signal as the Sergeant dug the heels of his shimmering feet into the dirt of the batter's box. The backstop motioned for me to throw one high and outside. I nodded my head and came into my set, peering out to the third base line as not to give my target away too quickly. As I drew into my motion, I said to myself,

"High and outside."

He hit that friggin ball so far, I thought it was going to come down somewhere in the pacific and sink a Japanese sub. I stood there, hands on my hips watching this thing fly, as everyone around me began to break into a roar. It was later explained to me that the Sergeant Major had spent time with another platoon before enlisting in the Marines. The Cleveland Indians. That made me feel a little better. Everyone seemed to have a good laugh at it so it is what it is or rather, was what it was.

There was this guy on the team by the name of Monte, and he came up to me toward the end of the season and said that I was a hell of an athlete and wondered if I'd be interested in playing basketball. I, of course, disagreed with his observation of my physical abilities. That said, I love basketball. I told Monte that, but I was much more honest with him about my experience with it . I had only played it a handful of times, in the gym at school when I was given the chance. Great game basketball is, great team game, and I love being part of a team. There's something about being around the guys, being around people, that's always grabbed me, and I liked the sound of being on an actual basketball team, with matching uniforms, playing in a nice clean gym. I told Monte I was in.

Now, in order for us to have a basketball team, we needed to practice. The problem was that we had no court to practice on, so Monte explained how we were going to get one. The Navy had just had a brand new, outdoor floor poured complete with two, state of the art hoops sitting ten feet off the ground on shining pipes. See, when you're on an island with multiple military branches it kind of morphs into a high school mentality in a way. The Army, well they're the jocks. The Marines are the coolest of the kids, and the Navy, well they are the lowest men on the totem pole. It wasn't because they were losers, or because they were any lesser men that we were. It was because the damn government gave them everything. They got new uniforms, new ships, new planes, new shoes, even new sports equipment.

We had a nice slab of concrete that would make a fine practice court for us. One night Monte and I went over to the Navy's side of the island, and measured the diameter of the poles that held the baskets high overhead. Upon our return we planted two pipes in the ground on either side of the slab, just a bit larger than the ones we'd just measured. One night later, about six of us drove over in a few trucks with a couple of saws, we mowed those poles down right at the bases, laid them in the beds of the trucks, and put them up on our slab. The next morning, those sailors came out with their starched clothes and gleaming balls to play and to their amazement, there was nothing there. The looks on their faces, priceless.

Unlike the baseball team, our basketball team was actually very good. We played as a team, as a unit, lots of ball movement trying to get the best shot. It was no wonder that a group of Marines would make for a great basketball team. We played everyone, Army, Air Force, Navy, and we beat them all, especially the Navy. We kicked the shit out of the Navy. One time they brought in a local team, native Puerto Ricans to play us. We suited up, warmed up, feeling pretty full of ourselves to be honest. God, they beat us six ways from sunday. At times I felt like they had seven guys on the court. We lost by twenty, which made it feel closer than it was. When there were no games to be played, it was still a good time. Do not get me wrong, we got screamed at, got punished, marched for hours and hours on end, but we weren't taking fire. We weren't in any real danger. I didn't wake up thinking that morning was going to be my last. I never saw Germans or Japanese lurking in the shadows. I was on an island. Plain and simple.

One weekend, we had about ten guys come in, all combat guys, and man they looked terrible. They couldn't eat or sleep. We stole a couple boats on a sunday morning, from the Navy or course, and armed with only a few bottles of rum, spent the day out on the water. The sun tanned our skin, making us look like vacationing beach bums, rather than

Marines. We sang songs, told jokes, I stood at the bow of one of the rafts and did my act, juggled, put some smiles on their faces. As someone who has been standing in front of people my whole life, those were the best laughs. Those guys, sitting in the boats, swigging that spiced rum, their shirts off and their heads back. They weren't seeing the faces of the friends they'd lost, they weren't seeing shores of bodies and crimson water, they were just having fun. They were free from all that, just like I had always been, at least for that moment.

My whole life, I always wondered what happened. Why was I spared? Not only my life, but my innocence, my rose colored view of the world. I was a civilian by 1948, and there were no sleepless nights, no flashes of light that made me jump. My wife and kids never had to hear me scream because of a dream or a memory. I have ten fingers and ten toes, two arms and two legs. The closest I've ever been to Japan was Hawaii, and closest to Germany was Florida. My military experience was never dramatized in films or television. I never fired my rifle or tossed a grenade at an enemy force, just tanned myself on the sand covered banks of the paradise in which I was placed. They shouldn't give awards to people like me. I drank and laughed and played while the real heroes, the real men lost parts of their minds, their souls and in some cases their lives.

So yea, I'll never wear that damn medal.

Building Six

Amanda jogged feverishly down the coastline, her dark brown hair tied-up behind her, the resulting tail whipping back and forth with each step.One foot after the other landing hard into the deep sand, each step strewing debris behind the young girl. Her thighs were really starting to burn now as she approached a fallen log, smoothed out by years of high tides. She planted her right foot firmly on the wood's surface and pushed off, sailing through the air and landing on her feet allowing her momentum to bring her into a forward roll. As she completed the rotation from her shoulder to her feet, she popped up and continued running, nary missing a stride. For years she had run on this beach, and it was those thousands of miles, her legs churning the sinking earth beneath her, that made Amanda Miller the athlete she was.

Queens Pointe was an idyllic place to grow up. Located on the southern coast of Massachusetts, it was one of the smallest towns in the state. Amanda mirrored the little village with her diminutive stature but she was indeed an individual who dwarfed her birthplace in both talent and spirit. She was just a few weeks removed from winning a

Division One High School Championship and the state competitions were just two weeks away. No one from Queens Pointe had ever won a Division Title let alone a State one, but Amanda knew she had a shot.

She stopped roughly, forcing herself to stand upright, her chest heaving in and out. She held her hand up to her neck and used two of her fingers to check her own pulse. As she breathed she stared down the beach at her home. Her Father had bought it only a few years after moving his family to the small, seaside town. Shortly after arriving, his law practice succeeded and he was able to move himself, his wife Anne, and his three-year-old daughter into a white, two-story Tudor home. Amanda's earliest memories were of strolling down the shore, her father on one side and her mother on the other. Those perfect days were not to last however, as Anne Miller was diagnosed with cancer just after her daughter's fifth birthday, and would succumb to the disease a few months later.

Turning from her home, she looked upward and faced the central landmark of her hometown. It was known as Building Six, of the old Queens Pointe Psychiatric Hospital, a brick and mortar structure that had an infamous past. Built in the mid 1930s, Queens Pointe Hospital was opened as a state-of-the-art facility dedicated to the treatment and study of mental Illnesses and patients. Its location on the shores of southern Massachusetts made it a sought after place to work for doctors and nurses. For almost 30 years the hospital operated like a fine oiled machine, the staff fully focused on their patients and duties during their shifts, and tanning and swimming in the waters of the coastline after hours. There were many buildings on the grounds but the largest and most impressive was by far, Building Six. Standing 13 stories high, the red blocked monstrosity resembled more of a hotel than a hospital. Its two towers were adorned with pale, cement angels, said to keep watch over the souls that dwelled inside.

In the fall of 1963, Queens Pointe Hospital was at its height, its huge buildings and beautiful grounds stood as a shining gem along the coast. Keeping a place that stunning required a lot of work, and of course, someone to do that work. In late September, a 25 year old, six foot three inch young man came to Queens Pointe. His wavy brown hair was shorn tightly at the sides. The long strands on top blowing in the salty air, sat above large, dark eyes which scanned his surroundings. His name was Sherman Marks, and he had come to Queens Pointe by way of his previous groundskeeping job at another hospital in Virginia. Upon his arrival, his tall frame and Southern charm quickly got him noticed by the young nurses that worked around the campus. On any given day when the sheer toting young man was clipping the many hedges that surrounded the buildings, scores of young ladies clad in white could be seen in the many windows staring at his strong arms protruding from his rolled up sleeves.

What most people at the hospital didn't know was that behind his chocolate eyes and Southern demeanor, Sherman hid a dark secret. Growing up, young Sherman was abused and tormented by his father about his weight. In the mid 1950s, the older Mr. Marks started feeding his son the diet pill called Obeterol. The medication's main ingredient was methamphetamine, which was not looked at as a dangerous substance at that time. The more weight Sherman lost the more pills he took, resulting in an eventual chemical dependency on the drug. After a while, the dosage wasn't enough for him and he needed another way to get larger amounts of amphetamines into his body. Now a full grown man, he got a job at a local hospital in his home state of Virginia. There he was able to have access to mass amounts of medications in the closets and cabinets that any hospital held. Eventually, the large quantities of missing narcotics became a glaring issue, and many questions were being thrown around as to their whereabouts. Under scrutiny and no doubt worried about his possible discovery, Sherman decided it was a good time to leave home, and he accepted a position at the

Queens Pointe Psychiatric Hospital in Massachusetts.

There was only one problem with his new place of employment. He now worked at a Psychiatric Hospital, which did not stock methamphetamines in the abundance he was used to. The only place for him to get what he needed was in the general medicine wing, on the first floor of Building Six. Everyday at lunch, the medical closet was monitored by one of two nurses. Marcie Allen was a statuesque blond who turned heads everywhere she went, and Grace Stanley, who was smaller and bespectacled, but every bit the head turner Marcie was. Both were native to the New England area, and had never heard the sultry sound of a tall, Southern boy's drawl. It didn't take long for Sherman to get into the routine of climbing the stone steps of the massive building, wandering down the long corridor and chatting with whichever of the two nurses were on duty that day. During the course of the conversation, Sherman would cover their station while whichever girl went to the restroom or to get something to eat. This allowed him the few minutes he needed to pilfer his medicine from the closet and place it into the pockets of his denim work overalls. As the weeks passed, the amount of pills he took increased. Seemingly everyday, his ticks and jitters from the previous dose's withdrawals would begin earlier and earlier.

On the 15th of November 1963, Sherman made his way down the hall of the east wing of Building Six. Marcie was standing by the closet, holding a clipboard and sorting the patients' various medications into their respective dosages. As the tall groundskeeper approached her she smiled, but then noticed that he didn't look as he usually did. His big brown eyes were sunken deep into his face, and he was sweating a considerable amount compared to the cool, autumn temperatures.

"Hey Sherm. You okay?" she asked.

"Oh yeah," Sherman sputtered, straightening his spine, "Just felt like taking a walk, wanted some better scenery."
Marcie's cheeks flushed as she covered her face with the tan piece of particle board she held in her hand. Sherman smiled back, the whole time looking past the nurse in front of him straight to the door which led to the real reason

for his visit. Thinking quickly, he
spoke again,

        "Hey, do you wanna ask the charge
nurse if you can take your break around
noon? Maybe we can get lunch."
Marcie blushed again as she raced down
the hall leaving Sherman in the doorway.
As soon as the girl was out of sight, he
spun around and opened the door. The
closet was small, barely two and a half
feet wide, with rows of drawers that
went from wall to wall and floor to
ceiling. Sherman ripped open the same
sliding box that he had for the last
several weeks and he was troubled by
what he saw. The pills had not been
replenished as he was consuming them
much quicker than the hospital was
re-ordering them. This meant that the
facility's inventory report didn't call
for a new shipment of the substance.
Grabbing the remaining tablets and
throwing them in his mouth, he turned to
the wall of drawers behind him which
held the liquid medications.

        Sherman had never thought about
taking his drug any other way but orally
but now, his sweating and shaking body
made him think about it. His twitching
right hand raised high about his head,
searching the labels on the wall in

front of him. His shivering finger came to land on a hand written label that read *C9H13NO3, Epinephrine*. He took the small glass vial out of the drawer and held it up to the light. He knew this wasn't his usual cocktail of medical pick-me-up, but he knew it would hit him much faster than the pills he'd just swallowed. He grabbed an empty syringe from the shiny metal container before him and drew out the liquid, he'd never done this before and unfortunately, it was later found that he had filled the needle with ten times the normal amount.

Poor Marcie walked in just as the adrenaline hit Sherman's heart. As soon as she had closed the door behind her, the tall groundskeeper wheeled around, the brown of his eyes almost gone, pushed aside by his rapidly expanding pupils. The half filled needle was still dangling from his bicep. Marcie tried to run but Sherman's long arm latched onto her and pulled her in close. Ripping the syringe from his own body he raised it high above his head and plunged it deep into the young nurse's neck, pushing the remaining contents into the girl. Marcie let out a scream as she threw back her head and arched her spine violently. Sherman clung to her lean, thrusting frame tightly, keeping it restrained until the motion stopped. Marcie's body fell to the floor, blood trickled from her nose as her eyes rolled back into her head so much that the shining blue circles became invisible. It would later be determined that her 21 year old heart had basically exploded from the high dose of adrenaline introduced to her system. Just as her body hit the tile floor, the closet door flung open.

Grace had been down the hall when she heard Marcie's frightening scream. Upon opening the store room door, she saw her friend crumpled on the floor, lifeless and bloody, the imposing Sherman standing over her with crazed eyes and gritted teeth. The smaller nurse let out a yell of her own, turning and running down the hall. Sherman set out after her, catching Grace just as she got to the main vestibul. Grabbing her by her short, curly hair, he pulled her into his arms. After a brief struggle, the male attacker got a hold of the teen's head, his massive hands on either side of her face. He jerked her off her feet quickly, snapping her neck, killing her instantly. Her twisted body hit the floor with a sickening thud echoing throughout the hall. Heaving air

in and out of his lungs, Sherman stood
hunched over, his hands on his knees,
his eyes dilated and fixed on the still
mound of flesh at his feet.

"Hey! Don't move!"

One of the Hospital's security guards
stood further down the corridor, his gun
drawn, the shaking barrel aimed in the
direction of the drug fueled
groundskeeper. Sherman stood tall for a
moment before running in the opposite
direction of the gun wielding officer,
towards the open doors. The first shot
rang out just as he hit the threshold
ripping through his lower leg. The
guard's second shot was fired from just
inside the building as Sherman tried to
limp away down the main stairs. It
struck him directly in the back of the
head. His body fell face down, between
the cement walkway of Building Six and
the row of hedges he had just trimmed
that morning.

Amanda bounded up the sandy hill on which Building
Six sat, her legs pulsing and pushing her small body up the
slope. Running up and down the slanting mound of grainy
sand had been a staple of her workouts for years. Often she
would end her trials by sprinting up the incline, placing her

hand on the fence that separated Building Six from the rest of the beach, then race back down. The hospital had been closed for almost 30 years, but most of the residents maintained that grounds were never the same after the events of November, 1963. As the years passed, the story of that day went from breaking news, to history, from history to folklore, then finally from folklore to legend. High School students would go up to the fence line of Building Six on stormy New England nights, and tell stories of Sherman Marks and his two young victims. The myth the children would spin was that no one ever dared go inside the perimeter alone, for they would be chased by the two nurses to the front steps of the structure where Sherman Marks waited to kill whomever trespassed.

Amanda touched the chain-linked fence as she always did and briefly looked through the cold, grey links to the decaying brick walls of the massive building. She began to turn her heels in the loose, dry dirt when she heard a sound. It was a loud single click, like the snapping of a twig or branch. As her head whipped in the direction of the noise, she thought she saw someone slip behind the corner of the building. Curious, the track star took a few steps down the enclosure, hearing only the sound of her feet in the sand, and the crashing waves in the distance.

Coming to the corner of the fence, Amanda froze. Inside the closed off area, between the walls of the immense hospital building and the chain-linked metal wall, walking slowly away from her, was a girl. In her whole life, she'd never seen anyone inside that fenceline, and it struck her in an unusual, queasy way,

"Hey!" Amanda called, "What are you doing?"

The girl inside the fence spun around, her blond hair turning with her dropping over her forehead. Amanda became even more uneasy as the mystery girl began to walk toward her. She was dressed all in white and she walked with uneven steps, blood was visibly dripping from her nose,

"Hey, are you alright?" Amanda called out again, simultaneously taking a small step backward.

The girl said nothing as she continued to stumble her way forward, finally lurching her body in Amanda's direction, bracing herself with one arm on the fence. Her face slowly turned up, revealing the parts of her face that had previously been hidden by her golden locks. Amanda's hand instinctively rose to her mouth as she could see the young girl's eyes, pristine orbital spheres of alabaster, bereft of any other color or marks staring right through her. The girl took in a sigh as she whispered two words that hung in the air like the wispy clouds that flew overhead,

"Help me…"

Just then, a silhouette appeared just over the frightening girl's shoulder. Amanda couldn't make out much of this second girl except for a pair of glasses on her face, glaring in the midday sun. No sooner did the second figure appear did she scream,

"Run! He'll get you too!"

Amanda tried to process what she was hearing and seeing. Her eyes drifted back to the bloody girl in front of her. The pair of hollow, white eyes locking with Amanda's narrowing brown ones. The ghastly looking blond in front of her pushed out a few words that sent a shiver down Amanda's spine,

"There's a hole in the fence."

Stumbling backward, Amanda's eyes began to dart from the two sun drenched figures inside the barrier to her side to side surroundings. Just as her heels touched the soft sand at the top of the hill the two girls behind the fence screamed in uniscion,
"Run!"
With that the Queens Pointe student turned and began to sprint down the steep incline she had ascended just moments before. Once at the bottom, she looked back and shielded her eyes from the intense sunlight above Building Six. Standing at the crest of the hill, towering the sand, was an enormous man. Amanda turned and ran down the shore, as fast as she could, back toward her house. Her breathing becoming so loud and frantic that it blocked out the sound of her own feet digging into the ground beneath her. Upon returning to her home, the out of breath girl screamed for her father, her body shaking from fear. When Mr. Miller heard his daughter's tale, he did everything to reassure her that she was in no danger, she was home, and she was safe.

Two weeks later, Amanda Miller won the Massachusetts State Championship in the 300 meter and 100 meter sprint. An article was published in the Queens Pointe Gazette about the local star and future Stanford bound athlete. It detailed her intense workouts on the shores of the bay which led to her crowning achievement, including the suicide sprints she would routinley do up a large sandy incline that led to the base of an old hospital building. It went on to be known as "Amanda's Hill," and many locals began trying to run the same sprints as their local High School hero. Unfortunately, not everyone can be as fit and gifted as Amanda. To this date, four people have died at the top of the hill. All four appearing to die from the same thing, their hearts exploding from the apparent strain, blood dripping from their nose...

Letter Of A Champ

    I don't know how much time I got, but I know it's not much. When you cross these men, they don't let you live it down. They don't let you live, period. I spent my whole life working and pleasing these men and now, with one mistake, I'm through. These scribbles are to let everyone know that I ain't never tried to do nothing less than what was asked of me, and I want my story known.

    I was born in Arkansas. I had 24 siblings and a father who hated every one of us who was too young or too weak to help work. I very much doubt that the person who finds this has any idea what it's like to work the fields, in the summer, in Arkansas, but it's murder. Even knowing my fate now, I still wouldn't go back there for anything. When that sun gets up in the sky, and the wind dies down, you wish you could shed your skin, just as you did your shirt, just to get some relief.

    When I was about 15 I think it was, our mule died. A mule in those days wasn't a pet, or a valued member of the family, but a tool, something to pull the load, a piece of farm equipment. My father used to hitch that old mule to the plow and work those rows, day in day out. When he finally dropped, we all thought he'd get a new one. We were right, and also, we were wrong.

What kind of a man, hitches his own son to a plow? The same kind of man that whips that son when he's not going fast enough, that's who. I still got the marks to prove it. I remember the leather ripping my skin like a fat man splits a pair of pants. At 15 years old I was treated like a farm animal by my own father. It wouldn't be the first time I was abused by someone. Maybe that was it. Maybe that was my problem. I got too used to it. Although all those other times was nothing compared to my father's hand at the whip. I would sleep on my belly so the night air would heal my cuts. Sometimes flies would land in the open wounds, although I'm not sure if that helped or not. It wasn't long after that I moved up north with my mother and my sister. Never saw my father again. Fuck him.

As much as I hated that farm, living in a big city was a big change. My mom got a job cooking in a kitchen and she challenged me to make money of my own. That was hard. Not many places or things I could do for a wage that was livable. I tried lots of labor jobs. Work that required a strong back and thick hands. I remember there was one day my boss decided he was going to make an example out of me. He tried to embarrass me. I knocked him on his ass right there in the street we was working on. Of course I was locked up. Pushing a white man to the ground is always frowned upon no matter where you live. If you ask me, no man should be pushed, white or black, but we all know that's never really going to be a universal idea.

Now when they let me out for that little tussle, there was a man waiting for me. The shine on his shoes was just like the shine on his hair. He had on this beautiful, grey suit with little sparkles in it. He looked like he was dipped in glass from head to toe. He said he had a job for me. He'd seen me push around that man and explained to me that he knew a few folks that owed him some money, and they needed a good shove too. I called him Sir, always.

My days became simple. I got a name and an address, and I went there to collect money. If they didn't pay, I did what I was told to do. When I got back, I was paid. That was it. My mother was impressed. I had me some nice clothes, had enough money to go to a nightclub, listen to music and dance with some pretty girls. That farm was a distant memory.

I wasn't all great. As I've come to learn, all swords, they got two sides. I was always having run-ins with the police. I mean more than normal. Sir always tried to keep me out as often as he could but there was only so much he could do. On my birthday I was sentenced to a year in jail for beating up a shop keep that owed about five grand to the men in the grey suits. They did what they could but all things considered, one year wasn't that bad. I was 18 when they closed the cell door for that first night.

Life inside wasn't the worst. It was simple. Just do what you're told and it was all fine. It was in prison that I first put on a pair of gloves. The leather was worn and cracked, much different than the ones I'd wear later, but they did the job. There was this priest inside, Father Stevens. He said I should learn how to box. That's when I was shown how to hold my hands, and how I should move my feet. Pretty soon there wasn't a guy in there that I hadn't beaten in the ring. Father Stevens thought I ought to get tested to see how good I really was. They brought in this man, Thurman Wilson I think his name was, they said he was a real pro fighter from the area. They brought him in and I all but murdered that man. I thought they might extend my sentence.

When I got out, the men in the grey suits sent me to philly to start really training. They introduced me to this guy named Willie Reddish. I fought for a while before they turned me pro, not more than a year or so. Anyone they put in front of me fell, they fell hard. It was beginning to feel easy again, only this time, no one locked me up for fighting, they celebrated me. This was a way I could become someone. Not only was I making money for the men in the grey suits, but I was making money for myself. The big thing I found out was when you walk into a bar or restaurant after you win a fight, they treat you different, they treat you better.

I kept winning. One after the other. I went in, I hit hard, and I got my hand raised, I got noticed. All of a sudden something became possible to me. I was beating top fighters, like I said, one after the other, and pretty soon the only one left for me to face, was the champ. Imagine that, me, fighting for the Heavyweight Championship of the World. The champ back then was a good little fighter named Floyd Patterson. He'd been to the white house, shook hands with the President. Picture that, a black man shaking hands, being admired, by the President.

The problem was Floyd's management, Cus D'Amato. Cus was one of the smartest boxing men that ever lived, and he knew that there wasn't a snowball's chance in hell that his boy could beat me. They told the press that the reason they wouldn't give me a shot was because of my background, my time in prison, my multiple arrests, my association with the men in the grey suits. Those men ran boxing, and now Floyd Patterson's camp wanted to pretend that their involvement was bad for the sport? Give me a fucking break. It went on like that for a long time until we were both booked on the same card. Floyd was fighting Tom McNeely, who was nothing, a warm body Cus lined up for him to beat on. I had to go against Bert Westphal who, let me tell you, was a damn good fighter. I left him laying on the canvas but still, a damn good fighter. After that night, everyone knew that I was the best heavyweight and Floyd, he was a paper champion.

After mounting pressure, Floyd finally told Cus he needed to give me a shot. It was the only way for him to hold on to any credibility whatsoever. They set the date and man, I never worked so hard in my life. They would have me stand straight up, and throw the heavy ball right into my belly. It got to the point where you could have fired a rifle at me and it wouldn't have done anything. This was the World Heavyweight Championship, there was no way I was going to leave anything to chance. Now I knew everyone loved Floyd, I just didn't know how much they hated me. When I walked into Comisky Park, it was like they were paid to boo. Meanwhile, Patterson, who beat nobody, was cheered like John Wayne.

When it came down to it, there really wasn't much of a fight. Although, I did not expect Floyd to come out swinging like he did. That's probably why he didn't last the round. Once you get inside, if all you do is try and hug me, it's not going to take long. When he took that ten count, I remember thinking this was it, my life was going to change. My corner rushed me and jumped and hollered, then I noticed the crowd. They were quiet, but not just crowd quiet, they were church quiet, funeral quiet. That should have been a tip off.

Flying back into Philly, I was nervous. I thought of all the questions I was going to have thrown at me. All the different papers that were going to want quotes from me, the new champ, for their evening editions. I couldn't wait to pick up the kids, hold them up high and smile for the pictures, making them feel just as good as I did. I thought about getting to shake hands with the Mayor or even a Senator, whomever was there. As the wheels touched down I looked over at Jack McKinney, a real newsman, and he gave me a pat on the knee. As I stepped off that plane I thought I was ready. I wasn't.

There was no one. Not one reporter. Not one fan. Not a soul. It hit me then, that it didn't matter. I was always going to be a thug, a brute who collected money for the men in the grey suits, and who got in dust ups with the cops. I worked my ass off, in spite of those things, in spite of it all. I came out of jail, trained, bled, sweated, and became the best, the Heavyweight Champion, and after all that, what did it do? What did it mean? Nothing. It did not matter one damn bit. Greatest country in the world.

After that, I didn't care. Despite what my own people said and told me, I felt slighted, and I think I ought have. I would go to dinner, and no one shook my hand, no one asked for an autograph, I wasn't even seated up front, I might as well have been a porter. A year went by and it was time for the rematch. I had to defend the title.

Time had passed, I had changed, but nothing was different. I was obviously still the better fighter, but Floyd was still beloved, he was looked at like a knight in a fable trying to slay the big, bad dragon. The bell rang and I almost took his head off of his shoulders, again. All in all, it lasted four seconds longer than the first time. At that point anyone that really knew boxing called me unbeatable, talked about me holding the title for 20 years, and other things like that. The rest of the country however, could not wait for me to fall. If I was shot in the ring, they'd turn a blind eye if it meant me losing that title. I was severely thinking about hanging it up, and calling it quits all together. Then came the Loud Mouth.

He was a tall, skinny boy from Kentucky. He was one of those kids that ran his mouth forever and never had anyone shut it for him. Now I really want to get something across to you. Everyone called me a bully, but that wasn't the truth. A bully just doesn't push you around, they embarrass you, they try to humiliate you. I knocked out Floyd's teeth, twice, but I left him with his dignity. The Loud Mouth was not like me, he wasn't just out to win, he was out for humiliation, he was the real bully. Around the time he showed up at my house, calling me names and forcing the police to make an appearance, I had made up my mind. I was going to kill Cassius Clay.

That night, I was ready, I got loose, got taped up, and put on my black hat. Right around when I was going out to the ring, I got a visit from a man in a grey suit. It turns out the Loud Mouth was an underdog. That wasn't a big surprise, but what was a surprise was the odds at eight to one. There's a lot of money to be made with odds like that. At first, I was of course against it. I hadn't been made to look like a fool for months so I can go in and lose to this asshole flapping his gums. Then it hit me. What was the point? I was an undefeated champ and they still hated me, so who would care about one loss? Plus if I was going to lose, I might as well make money off of it. I thought about it and made the decision. I was going to lose, line my pockets, and get him at the rematch.

I took some punches, let him cut me, did my part. Apparently someone in my corner didn't get the message and loaded my gloves up with the Monsel's Solution, almost blinded the guy. I even heard him yelling at his corner to cut the gloves off cause he couldn't see. That would have fucked everything up. After that round I decided, no more chances, I was done. I sat down on that stool and told them it was over, I couldn't continue. It was called cowardly, not getting up off the stool. Champions were supposed to go down swinging they wrote. All I kept thinking was, now they considered me a champion? Wonderful timing.

As expected, I cleared a lot of cash from that fight. Enough to get me that nice house in Vegas on the golf course. I would go to the club and see Sinatra, Joe Louis, or other guys from the strip, and shoot craps at night. It felt good to be a loser. It almost felt bad to know that I was going to have to take the title back and go back to being the champion.

A funny thing happened though, on the way to the rematch. The Loud Mouth joined the nation, can you believe that? He took on a new name and joined the most outspoken, violence based religion in the country. It's hard enough to be black in this country, but now you're going to be black and radicalized? He would have been better off beating up cops like me. The thing was now, all of a sudden, it was him that was the hated one. I seemed like the hero, imagine that.

As I got ready to murder a man in front of a live crowd, I really began to like having not only the press, but the people in my corner for once. Maybe this was the time, my time. I would finally be treated like the Champion. Like I should have been treated before. I got this glow over me around that time. I was in a city that I liked, I had a little money and a house in a neighborhood with other famous people in it, and I was going to be the champ that everyone loved, finally. I couldn't stop smiling.

About a week before the fight, I was approached again. The odds, predictably, were against him, and they wanted to make some more dough. It was always about money. This time I flat out refused. It was time to shut his mouth, get back my title, my respect. It was time for me to be cheered, to be celebrated. I told the men in the grey suits that there was no amount of money, no deal that would be able to change my mind. Once again, I was wrong.

This was the offer. I was going to get a piece of every one of Loud Mouth's future fights. Whatever he was paid, I had a cut. I was basically going to own him. That's how I would get my dignity back from him, owning him, literally. I could go on earning money long after I hung my gloves on a nail and put my feet up. After much talking and thinking, I shook hands on the deal.

When I stood in that ring in Lewiston, I was cheered. It killed me. It made me sick in my belly. I wanted to embrace it, to love it, but knowing what I was about to do, it just killed me. As they called my name I just raised my hand and hung my head. I knew that was the closest I was ever going to get to being what I thought I always should have been, an inspiration. I felt so shitty when they rang that bell, I just wanted it to be over. He came out, dancing like he did, moving left and right. He connected with a powder puff, little nothing left. I went down onto my back. He stood over me, yelling at me, calling me all the names he did. I just rolled to my belly.

The booing started and I thought, I had to get up, find a better place to do this. When I sat up, I could see the crowd. I could see their faces. I could see the hate. Fuck them. This was all they were going to get. I rolled back onto my belly.

After that night, although I continued to get fights, I was never considered a contender. I wasn't surprised. That was what I agreed to with the deal I made. I would fight bums and most of the time I had to knock them out. After that rematch dive, everyone thought I was a has been, so the odds were always against me. It paid to have me win now, so the men in the grey suits wanted me to win, and so I did. I did what I was told, always.

Lower level fights though, paid lower level money. I went back to my roots, collecting money for some dope dealers on the west side of Vegas. That's where I've been hanging out mostly. The strip people just laughed and teased me about the losses and called me a coward and a bum. The west side people were my people though, and they understood that what I had done was something to be respected. They're good people, despite their demons. Can you imagine? Me coming into a bar to knock your teeth down your throat cause you owed a few hundred dollars to a red headed trumpet player who sold you some shit? This country, I tell you, just crazy.

In between fights and collecting, I played craps. You know something, in all the noise, the machines, the people yelling and screaming, all the usual ruckas that happens at casinos, I found craps soothing. Everyone at the table, backing the guy with the dice, the guy with the hot hand. Scooping up those red cubes on a good streak, the other players patting you, being with you. The elation when those white dots turn up just right is pure joy. I smile with the dice. Of course I've had my cold runs too. When the dice are cold, its isolation.

I remember I was eating at the Stardust, in this little cafe, and I had just put down a little money for the waiter and this writer came around. Izenburg I think his name was. He was in town for another fight and we hadn't seen each other in awhile. He asked after me and I, of him. We just stood there and chatted for awhile, which I enjoyed, and I asked him if he'd eaten. He told me he hadn't. I told me I hadn't either, so we sat down and ate.

Needless to say, I was in a pretty low place when they asked me to take on Wepner. He had been some type of soldier boy before he became a fighter. The men in the grey suits wanted him to win. A win over a former champion was going to set him up for a big time fight, and more importantly to them, big time money. It sounded easy enough, but little did I know that I'd find myself where I am now, inking my last words onto a few scraps of paper I found on the floor of a leaky locker room.

I know people are going to ask questions, so I need to explain what happened. The problem was that the last dive, the Loud Mouth rematch, looked too bad. People started yelling fix as soon as the bell sounded. I needed this one to look good. I threw a jab and the son of a bitch didn't move. I got him right above the eye and cut him deep. Now, it wasn't like I could just stop throwing punches, and dammit, every time I landed one this guy would open up again. It looked like a scene from a riot. It was a mess. As he bled, he stopped throwing punches. There was no place for me to fall. It was just a matter of time before they called it cause this guy was bound to pass out from leaking. I just don't know what I was supposed to do. How dumb do you have to be to lose a fixed fight?

These men, they don't like when things don't go according to plan. Even I'm smart enough to know that. Now I have a few moments left. I could have done more had I been given a fair shake. It sounds unusual saying that. A boy who was hitched to a plow and whipped by his father, goes to prison, comes out of that to become the Heavyweight Champion and still didn't get a fair shake. I didn't. I just didn't. The truth is, I was never THE Champ. I was just A Champ. This country…

I hear yelling coming down the tunnel. Heavy footsteps from shiny shoes are echoing all around me. I hope this letter finds you, someone, anyone. I done my best. I tried.

Sonny Liston.

The Old Man

The Old Man awoke, his head still groggy, the sight in his eyes slowly clearing from their haze. He was in a small room, whose details were unfamiliar to him. His glasses seemed to be missing making it even harder to make out his surroundings. The walls were coated in peeling rows of ink and paper. A hard, dark floor, the shade of wine, was beneath his feet. There was a small window to his right which was open, the outside gusts causing the white linen curtains to billow into the room, much like a matador's cape. The bed at his side was sheeted in dark flannel, the top blanket a raging fire like color, the sight of which shocked his system into total awareness. He attempted to rub his eyes only to find that his hands were bound to the wooden chair in which he sat. His ankles were also tied to the dark oak legs with thick, coarse twine. His belt had been used to attach his torso to the middle of the seat, although the most troubling thing perhaps, was the fact that he was also completely naked.

Last he had remembered, he had been playing in a small park with his granddaughter. She had been sitting in the grass, plucking at the flowers, her blond hair drifting in the wind. He suddenly realized that he had no idea not only where he was, but if she was safe. Now he began to thrash and strain, trying to free himself from the ropes. It was then he heard someone move behind him. The unknown figure walked with heavy steps upon the solid floor, his breathing was slow and controlled, in sharp contrast with that of the Old Man's. Without revealing himself, the looming shadow leaned over and whispered into his ear,

"Good morning,"

It was then he came out from the hiding place behind the captured man.

The Old Man's eyes widened as he saw an enormous fellow, clad in dark pants and a pristine, white shirt come around and position himself directly before him. His buttons were only done halfway up, allowing his full neck to be exposed and the numerous scars it bore to be visible. The towering man had dark hair, with eyes to match. They pierced the Old Man's soul and he just stood there, silent for what seemed like minutes. Finally, his captor spoke again,

"It took me years to find you."

His language was familiar, but the accent that came with it seemed very foreign.

"I am going to allow you to tell me why you should live, and when you are finished, I will tell you why I'm still going to kill you."

Shocked and dumbfounded, the Old Man stared in silence while the larger and younger of the two sat himself in a chair, lit a cigarette and patiently awaited a response. Writhing in his ropes, he fumbled and wheezed as he tried to comprehend the whole situation, the details of which seemed impossible. Somewhere in his mind he believed it was all a dream, that he would wake up again, this time in his home or perhaps he was still in the park, napping next to his granddaughter. Years ago, during the war, he had often been able to wake himself from nightmares by closing his eyes tightly and forcing them to reopen. He tried this now, but to no avail.

" I'm waiting," the large man hissed through the smoke.

"Please," he started, "Please. I'm just an old man. I do not know who you are or who you think I am. I beg you."

"Why? Tell me why I should let you live."

"I have not harmed you. That is why."

" That is technically true. You have not harmed me."

"Well then," the Old man bellowed, " That is why. That is why!"

The dark haired figured leaned back in his chair, thinking as he drew once again on the smoldering stick between his fingers,

"No. It's not about me. I want to know about you. Tell me about the girl in the park."

The Old man gasped, thinking that maybe he wasn't the only one in the danger,

"That is my Granddaughter! Please! I beg you!"

"Calm yourself," he exhaled, "I'm not the monster."

The Old Man momentarily breathed relief,

" Her name is Ilse. I take her to the park on Sundays after church. She loves the colors of the flowers."

"Such a good man you are. It's so nice when children can grow up with the love of a Grandparent."

The Old Man began to speak with fervor,

"Yes! That is why you must not do this! Please. My Grandaughter, little Ilse, with her perfect gold hair and eyes the color of the sky. Please. Who will take her to the park? Who will bring her to see the flowers?"

The man who sat opposite him only stared as he rolled up the right sleeve of his shirt. He took the butte of his cigarette and dabbed the cherry colored end into his massive forearm. His expression never changed as he then inched his chair closer to the Old Man,

"What about her parents?"

"My daughter Emma cannot take her on Sundays. She has to work."

" So you have children?"

" Yes, just her. My Emma. She has been the joy of my life."

" Keep going."

The Old Man took a moment to reflect on the small German town he and his wife had settled in,

"After the war my wife and I just wanted to forget. We found a small town away from the city where no one knew our names. There was a little farmhouse with a creek in the field next to it that we decided to make our home. We both worked at the train station in the town. My wife took tickets and I would keep the trains on schedule, much like I did when I was a soldier."

"Well that sounds like a nice little life you guys had."

"Yes it was. When Emma was born we thanked our Christian God for the gift of a healthy child. We gave her all the love that our parents didn't give to my wife and I."

"Yes," the man sighed, "I do know something about not getting the love one deserves from a parent."

The Old Man implored,

"Then you see, you understand. I need to live, for my daughter, for my wife, for my family."

The heavy listener folded his arms, unimpressed,

"Your daughter Emma is married? Was there a wedding?"

"Oh yes, a beautiful wedding."

"Tell me about it, What did she look like that day?"

" Oh she was a vision, a sight to behold," he started, "Her hair was in curls, the color of the sunlight, hanging just above her shoulders. I remember watching her walking in the church, her hands clutching beautiful flowers. My wife held me as we both gave her away. That was a good day,"

He stopped, as he began to feel tears build in his eyes. He hadn't thought of that day in a long time.

"I imagine you felt grateful that day. Grateful for your wife, your daughter, for life."

"Yes," the old man sobbed, "I was. I am. I want nothing more than to see them again. To See my Emma smile. To hold little Ilsa. To touch my wife's cheek."

With this the tears broke free from his eyelids and began to stream down his face and onto his naked body. His breathing became frantic and labored. He again tried to pull and break free from the ropes and chair he was shackled to. The man before him leaned forward, and placed a large palm onto his shoulder,

" Okay," he whispered.

"What?"

The giant rose from his seat, and reached behind the bed. He produced a small, leather bag which had been hidden on the floor,

"You have told me why I should let you live."

The Old Man looked up with hopeful eyes,

"Yes I did. Now you will let me go?"

Planting himself back into the empty seat, he spoke,

"No. Now I will tell you why I am going to kill you," he said as he reached over and unzipped the bag which sat on the bed next to him.

His thick, heavy hand produced a small picture from within the satchel. Moving deliberately, he held the photo up close for the Old Man to see. It was an image of a young soldier, with bright eyes looking into the distance, his uniform freshly pressed,

"This is you, yes?"

The Old Man recognized his younger self and nodded his head slowly. The photo was then placed back into the bag and the large man began to roll up his left shirt sleeve,

"You said you used to keep trains on schedule when you were a soldier. Well, what if I told you," he leaned forward again, extending his newly uncovered arm, " That I was on one of those trains."

The Old Man gasped as he looked upon the mass of flesh and muscle, in which six crooked numbers were crudely etched upon the skin in faded black ink.

"I do not think I need to say anything more to you, but I have been waiting for this moment a very long time. My name is Adler. My family was among the first to arrive on one of your trains. We stood in a long line, holding each other's hands not knowing anything about what was going on. Then, I can remember it as clear as a cloudless sky, there you were, in your stunning uniform. You looked at us as you would a coat or hat or any other inanimate object. Without a word you ripped me from my family and pointed for them to go off in another direction. When I tried to follow them, you drew a large knife and held it to my throat, cutting me a little, giving me the first of many marks," he gestured towards one of the scars on his neck, "You told me I would always be little and weak. Do you remember me?"

The Old Man hung his head, unable to answer. Adler lurched forward, grabbing the wrinkled face in front of him and forcing his eyes to meet his own,
"I said, do you remember me?"
Tears again began to fall down the Old Man's cheeks,
"No!" he cried.

He pushed the man's head back,
" Of course you don't. You probably said that countless times. None was more meaningful than the other."
He sprang forward once more, snatching his former tormentor by the neck,

"I never saw them again. You sent them to their death," Adler said through tensed whispers, "There were no homes to be made. No more children to be had. No weddings to attend. No flowers to be seen. You took all of that from them. You took all of that from me. You took all of that from thousands!"

The Old Man bellowed,
"No! It wasn't me! I was a soldier! I was just doing what I was told!"
Adler squeezed tighter around the man's throat,
" You pointed. You. It was you."
He relinquished his grip and shot up from his seat, the chair behind him falling backward to the floor. In one motion he ripped his shirt from his body, revealing the true immense size of his frame. He stood there, both arms held outward,
"Tell me. Do I look little? Do I look weak?"
The Old Man shook his head, sobbing as he spoke,
"No."
The young man put his arms down,
"You told me that after the war you wanted to forget, and by all accounts you made a really solid effort to try, but you and I both know the truth. We know that no one can ever forget the kind of monster you are, the kind of horror you allowed to happen. You can shed your tears about Emma, and Isla and the flowers all you want but when I look into the eyes that are crying those tears, I can see one true thing."
"What," the Old Man wheezed.
"You knew this day was coming."

Adler took several heavy steps to the open window and, with one hand, slammed the wood framed glass down, sealing it tight. He then turned his attention back to the brown, leather bag that lay upon the bed.He whipped back around and the Old Man looked in horror at what he had produced. The fingers of his left hand were wrapped around a large, silver canister. The labeling had been etched off but he had seen canisters like it before. He knew it, because his fellow soldiers had dropped thousands of them down small pipes into sealed rooms years prior. In his right hand, Adler held a rubber mask, with large glass covered eye holes, and a long, snout-like protrusion. The Old Man became frantic. Pulling and thrashing in his chair he began to scream causing the veins in his neck to bulge and his voice to crack,

"No! God, no! Please! I beg you!"
The man before him stared with lifeless eyes, the panicked cries falling on deaf ears. He watched and listened as the screams turned to wails, grunts and other guttural emissions. In one motion he thrust the mask over his head and pulled it into position.

"What's the difference!" the old man screamed again, his eyes clamped shut.

Adler paused, then spoke from beneath his leathered mask,
"Excuse me?" he asked, his voice muffled.
Once again the old man shrieked,
"What's the difference?" he asked, his eyes still closed, unable to face what was standing before him, "You are doing what you think I did to you? It's monstrous! It makes you no better!"

Adler shifted his mask off of his face so that it sat on top of his head,

"What's the difference?" he repeated.

He lurched at the man, his large hands grabbing each of the captured wrists, which were still lashed to the arms of the chair. Adler's jaw tensed, he glared into the closed eyelids of the shivering elder,

"If I wanted to do the same to you that you did to me, I would," he started, "I would take this mask and place it on your face. Then I'd open that door, and march that little girl right in here…"

The Old Man's eyes shot open, his face only inches from Adler's, the huge man continued,

"I'd stand here right here, then make you watch here die."

The two just glared into each other's eyes,

"But you know what?" Adler said, calming his voice, "If I did do that, take the life of a child. You'd be right, exactly right. That is exactly what a monster would do."

He leaned forward a bit more, so that their noses were virtually touching,

"I'm just going to take your life. One life, onelife in exchange for thousands," Adler whispered,his hot breathe falling upon the old man's skin, "And your life, the life of a monster, the life of a Nazi… is still a life."

He eased backward, taking his hands off of the tied wrists,

"And when my time comes and I face judgment," he said, holding out his self mutilated arm for the Old Man to see, "As your faith would say, I am fully prepared to burn for it… That, that is the difference."

The man in the chair had no response, he just stared,his face gone. Adler reached up and pulled the mask back over his face and tightly gripped the metal can. Through the stiff rubber he offered just a few more words for the Old Man,
    "I'm going to watch you die."
With that, he raised the canister high above his head and, with all his strength, threw it to the ground, smashing it on the floor.

The Provider : On The Road

New York City always seemed like a far away land to me. I would come down the parkway to visit my father in Yonkers, and see the buildings rising from the water with the glittering lights and the vibrating sound setting my senses on fire. I imagine a kid having the same feeling when they first see Disneyland from a distance. When I was in the service, everyone always heard I was from New York, and they always assumed that meant the city. The truth is that Hudson was the furthest thing from Manhattan in every way imaginable. The one hotel, the one library, the one cafe, and the three bars. Manhattan had all of that in less than half a block. When I got out of the Marines I was home for all of three minutes before I realized that I couldn't stay there. I wasn't going to spend my life staring at the same brick buildings, on the same cement streets, with the same cobblestone curbs.

My last night in my home town was something I tell ya. There was this bar that I used to work at from time to time. I went in there for a few farewell drinks, which turned into more than a few, which turned into me being behind the bar juggling bottles and doing some of the old tricks. There was one that particularly amused people where I would make all the contents of a tumbler disappear right before their very eyes. Now before you jump to conclusions, the answer is no, I did not just dump the alcohol into my mouth. It was just the simple act of putting a dry dish rag into the bottom of the stainless steel canister. Once the liquid was poured into it, the towel absorbed the cocktail and when I turned the tumbler over, there was nothing left to do but take in the applause. When I think back on it, I really do miss those times.

The following morning it's natural that I was a little slow, and as I was making my way to the bus station, I ran into a friend, Pat, who I'd known for years. He told me he'd heard I was leaving or, as he put it, making a break for it. I told him I was and before I knew it he had his hands outstretched in front of me,

"Can you wait a little bit? I'm coming with you. I need an hour. All I need is an hour."

An hour later, as I stood next to the shining, silver Greyhound, he came running, suitcase in hand. As we boarded the bus, I asked him what he had needed the hour for? His response still gets me everytime I think about it,

"I needed to sell my car."

Manhattan was everything I had always thought it would be. The sounds of the honking cabs, the smell of the food from the restaurants, the people all walking like they had someplace to go. I looked like the stereotypical country bumpkin, neck arched, my eyes wide, trying to see the tops of the buildings. Walking down the streets, my companion and I popped into and out of many bars. I mean, there were dozens of them just in the theater district alone. Now that was amazing. Broadway, I mean. The lights, the marquees, the energy. I thought about what it must be like to perform on proper stages like that. How heavy, and thick the curtains must be. How blinding the footlights supposedly were.

The specifics of that night are long forgotten, but two things I remember for certain. The first is that I did a handstand on the ledge of the 12th floor of the New Yorker Hotel. Everytime I'm asked why, I always say the same thing,
    "Because I could."
The truth is, I had a lot of help from my friend, Jack Daniels. The second memory I have of that night, is where we slept. Now, a hotel room cost a few dollars back then, which was way more than we wanted to spend, so we each bought a ticket to the movies. Pictures were shown all night and the cost of admission was only ten cents, that's how I spent the night sleeping in the plush, red seats of the Amsterdam Theater.

The next morning we went down to Grand Central Station. I had picked out Dayton, Ohio as the next stop. I knew a bunch of guys from the service who lived in Dayton and figured I could go there and find some work. The ticket to Dayton cost thirteen dollars. Pat tapped a bit on my shoulder,
    "How much is the ticket?" he asked.

"Thirteen," I said.

"Great. Can I borrow Thirteen dollars?"

Pat was broke, after one night.

When we got to Dayton, I went right to my friend Monte's house. He was gone unfortunately for us, but his elderly mother offered us a room to rent. It wasn't much, one room, two beds, a small table and a phone. It was a start but I knew that we needed to get moving. Needless to say by the time we got to Ohio I was now broke as well. Pat and I found this bar where you could play Uker. We developed a series of hand signals to let each other know what we were holding. The bar paid out in tokens that you could use for drinks or food, no cash payouts, but that's how we ate and survived those first few weeks. We did find some odd jobs here and there and were able to save a tiny bit but it wasn't nothing substantial.

Now craps. Craps was a way to make a small amount of money into a virtual king's ransom. I've never been much of a gambler but I did like the idea of having a good time and making a little money at the same time. Pat had heard through the grapevine that there was a little house outside of Dayton that we could roll some dice. Pat always had a way of talking me into things. By the time we walked up to the house, he had me convinced that this night was going to be profitable in more ways than one.

As we walked through the door I started to doubt my own thoughts. The place was lit up bright. Yellow fabric covered the walls and every window had gorgeous dark red drapes. Each drape was covered in tassels and I remember thinking how elegant the whole place looked. The first thing I saw after the walls and tassels were the women. There were about a dozen amazing looking girls, all lined up, make-up and hair done perfectly. In front of them was an older lady, wearing a beautiful dress and smoking a cigarette. She was in the process of introducing another man to one of the girls...

…. A brothel. We were in a brothel.

Pat was right though, there was a craps table. We got standing around and playing within no time. The drinks were flowing and we put everything we had on the table. There a young guy standing next to us, a black guy. He went right up to Pat,
"Hey, I know you."
Pat turned, taking his eyes off the table for a split second,
"From where?"
"Albany."
Pat huffed a little bit,
"Where in Albany?"
"The Wilshire Hotel."
Pat let out a burst of laughter,
"You're full of shit. They don't let niggers in there."
I died. Now I was never the most well spoken guy when it came to these matters, but I would never flat out use language like that, just seems wrong. It felt like time stood still for that fleeting moment until the guy whom Pat had insulted burst into laughter and gave him a slap on the back.

That was the only positive feeling from that night. We lost almost everything, and just as the young black kid got on the table and looked to be hot with the dice, we heard a crash from downstairs. It sounded like the front door exploded and then hoards of screams and hollers came up the stairs. The place was being raided, can you believe that? Cops, complete with their night sticks and guns came flooding up from the first floor. I grabbed Pat by the arm and ran to the closest open window,

"John there's no way."

I pushed his head down and out into the night air,

"We don't have a fucking choice, now jump."

There we went, both of us, out the second story window. Luckily though, the ground broke our fall.

We started walking back to Dayton. I pulled my collar up and realized my overcoat, the one I'd been issued in the service, was on the back of a chair in that whorehouse. It's probably still there.

Ohio was cold. It was really cold. The lady we were renting from seemed to really like me, but we could only stretch that so long, so we needed to find some work. Pat and I would each take a bus in opposite directions, looking around to see where or who was hiring. After a particularly cold and frustrating day or searching, I plopped myself down on the hard seat of the return bus home. Leaning my head against the frigid glass window, I closed my eyes trying to forget the fact that I had spent my last dime on the fare for this greyhound bullet. It was then that I felt someone standing over me.

I opened my eyes to see a striking blond, bound in wool and cotton, looking down at my raggedy self,

"Excuse me, do you mind if I sat with you?" she said with a smile.

"Of course not," I chirped back, pulling on my sportcoat, trying to make myself look less pathetic than I did.

I scooted over to let her in, knowing that whether or not this went the way I thought it could, that I'd at least get a little warmth from having another human being sitting in the seat with me. She quickly made conversation by telling me how obvious it was that I wasn't used to the midwestern winter weather. I let her know that I had spent the previous two years in Puerto Rico, and that I had never felt my eyelids freeze before. We continued on like that. I made her laugh and she was pretty damn funny too.

When we arrived at the station in Dayton, I turned my collar up against the wind and looked into the eyes of my traveling companion. As I was planning my parting line, she asked me something I was not expecting,

"Hey, do you want to go get some coffee?"
My stomach sank as I knew that I didn't have the money for that. I mean, I didn't have the money for anything. I gave her a smile and took in a breath,

"Sure let's go"
I'm an idiot.

We soon found ourselves in a cozy little booth of the diner across the street from the bus station. The waitress came around and I quickly let her know that I was just going to be getting a coffee. To my horror, the girl who sat across from me began to order a full lunch or roast beef, potatoes, vegetables. She peered over the menu and pleaded with me,

"You're really not going to get any food?"
What was I supposed to say? I gave my shoulders a shrug and blurted out an order of sausage and eggs. I can't tell you how the food was or what we talked about while we were eating, because all I could think about was how the hell I was going to get out of this.

The waitress might as well have been carrying an ax as she walked to our table to deliver the check. It had hardly touched the table before the girl sitting before me snatched it and paid the entire thing. I sat, dumbfounded and embarrassed, trying to find words to make me seem not thoroughly relieved.

"Hey, ya know, I just moved here and I'm really closer to finding work. Once I get my first paycheck I'll give you a call and we can go out again and I'll repay you for lunch."

She gave me a smile and a laugh, and told me that her name was Marie Jones, and gave me her phone number.

After we parted ways, I made the two mile walk back to the house where we were staying. Pat was sitting in our room reading when I walked in. He shot off his bed as if he was on a spring and grabbed me by both shoulders,

"I did it! I found us some jobs!" he shouted.

I couldn't believe it,

"What? Where?"

" A few miles away, at the Asylum, as orderlies! We start monday!"

My hand pulled out the number I had scribbled out only an hour before and I reached for the phone. I could hardly dial the numbers. I was so excited. I was going to have a job, and possibly a girl. This day was turning around quickly. A female voice answered the phone,

'Hey! How's It going," I started, "Its John, I'm calling for Marie."

The woman on the end of the line paused for a second,

"Marie? Marie Jones?"

"Yea that's the one," I laughed.

"We get phone calls for that girl all the time, we've never heard of her."

The receiver clicked off and I set it down upon the desk. Apparently there's a girl in Ohio who rides a bus, finds a guy, takes him to lunch, gives him a fake name and number, and never sees that guy again. I turned back to Pat who was still grinning from ear to ear,

"Wait a second," I said, " Did you say, an Asylum? Like a mental hospital?"

Pro Wrestling

I was eleven years old and I sat myself down on a saturday morning. I turned on the old Zenith and as the glass hummed and warmed up and the picture came into focus, I saw a huge man, biggest I've ever seen, standing next to a suit gentleman holding a microphone. He wore a mask over his face and waved his massive finger at me through the screen. He spoke in a loud, gravelly voice, and told everyone that he was going to commit a crime in the ring this tuesday. He then spat on the floor and walked out of frame. The next shot I saw was that of a small, canvas covered ring, surrounded on all sides by ropes. The large man then jumped through those ropes and proceeded to beat the holy hell out of a much smaller man who had already been standing there. AS he stood over the beaten body, he had barely broken a sweat, and i could hear the announcer screaming over the gasps and yells of the crowd that had just witnessed the mismatch,

"The Crusher takes on the King this tuesday! Will this be a sign of things to come? We will find out this tuesday! Get down here, you are not going to want to miss this!" I was already up and off the couch, tugging at my mothers dress, begging her for tickets. I was hooked, just like that.

Pro Wrestling was probably the most uniquely American way to make a living. Where else but America can you sell the illusion of combat to the masses for their own entertainment? I came into the business at a time when the fans thought that everything we did was very much real, and if anyone even suggested otherwise, they would be dispatched physically. My God, I worked for promoters who, if you didn't fight when someone said wrestling was fake, you got your notice. We now live in a time where all of our most guarded secrets have been revealed and nothing provokes a general reaction from fans anymore. When I was working, peop-le would scream and faint when their favorite athlete was dropped, headfirst, onto the mat. Nowadays, I literally saw some bastard light himself on fire, and there was a guy in the front row sitting. I'm only writing this to show how real it was and to proclaim, once and for all, that Pro Wrestling is dead. Once Dorothy peers behind the curtain, she cannot unsee the Wizard.

I am first and foremost a believer that in order to truly love this business, you must have first been a fan of it. Too many times have I worked with someone who got into wrestling because they had a great look or failed at another sport. Many times those types of guys never amount to much. It's the fans that grow up to be the headliners and main events.

I made my living as a Manager. I would accompany a wrestler to the ring and do his talking for him and aid him in any way that I could. I was a bad guy in wrestling, which we called a "heel." More often than not, whoever I was managing was always opposite a good guy, or a "face," or "baby face." Just typing this makes me want to vomit. To think of all the broken bones that were mended in defense of this knowledge. As for my job specifically, I was responsible for getting the crowd to hate me, me and whoever I was managing. A typical night for me started with standard boos and hisses, and ended with screams, slurs, and if I was extra good, maybe even an attempted assault. Like I said, American.

Nowadays, there's really only one place to work in Pro Wrestling. When I was active, there were dozens of promotions spread out over the entire country known as Territories. On this particular night, I was working in an area known as the Mid-South Territory. The promoter I worked for there was the legendary Bill Watts. Most people don't know his name today, but he was one the greatest wrestling minds that ever lived. He was a phenomenal athlete when he was younger, and started in both football and wrestling at the University of Oklahoma. He was such a natural to the business of Pro Wrestling that he was headlining Madison Square Garden in just his second year in the business. As the 1970's came to a close, Watts bought majoprity ownership of the Mid-South Territory and quickly showed that his instincts were not limited to in ring action, but extended to the box office decisions as well.

I started out as, what was known back then, as a ring second. My Mother, who took me to the matches every Tuesday, was a charming woman. She made friends with some of the office people and got me the job. All I had to do was take the werstler's and jackets from thema s they entered the ring and walk them back towards the locker room. I want it to be known that I was not allowed into the actual locker room themselves, that was a sacred place. I did that until I was about fifteen, then I got my first camera.

It;s hard to become a wrestling photographer, or at least it was back then. I first just started asking some of the boys if they wanted me to take their picture. I told them they could use it as their headshot or their adverts or even send it into the magazines. It wasn't long before some of my work got noticed and actually placed into a few of those magazines and even began selling at the merchandise tables. I was asked one day if I wanted to shoot some stuff down in the front by the ring and there I was, a real ringside photographer. I got to take pictures and see some of the greatest matches, up close and personal. There were some nights when the sweat and blood from the combatants would stain my clothes. I was so close, and I thought that life couldn't get any better than that.

Shortly after my eighteenth birthday, I was approached by the man himself, Bill Watts. He said he wanted to sit me down and talk a bit. I remember sitting across from him, his hulking frame spilling out over the edges of the chair, telling me how great a job he thought I was doing with the pictures. That's when he said it,

"So," he said, "It's come to my understanding that you're smart to our business."
Over the years, watching it as much as I had, being as close to it as I was, I figured it out. I knew the secret without being told, but I had never let that be known. I froze. I didn't know what to say. I was always afraid that if anyone knew I was

smart, as they called it, that they'd cast me out, send me away, and that would have killed me,

"Why," I stammered, " I'm not sure what you mean, Sir."

Watts leaned in a bit,

"It's okay Son," he said, "I know, you know."

Devastated, I nodded my head slowly.

"Well, listen Son," he said, leaning back in his chair, "I've heard you speak, and I think you have quite the motor mouth on you. What do you think about being one of our managers?"

Needless to say I was relieved, and needless to say, I accepted the offer. I became a wrestling manager in the Mid South Territory at the tender age of nineteen.

When I was there I was managing a guy called, The Masked Viper. Now The Viper, or "Vipe" as I call him, was a pretty big guy for the time. He was about six foot five inches tall and weighed around two hundred and sixty pounds. The problem with him was, despite his size, he had one of the highest, squeaky voices one has ever heard. Watts wanted The Viper to work on top (that means he wanted him to wrestle the most important matches). He took me, the skinny kid from Arkansas with a bamboo cane, and made me the giant mouthpiece. We had been paired together for a few months when we made our way to the ring on that muggy tuesday night. We were just outside New Orleans so even though we were still indoors, you could feel the humidity in the building. It was almost like the air was so thick you could chew it. When we walked out, we always went out the same way. Vipe was in front and I was slightly behind, holding my can on the shoulder with the curved part of the handles right next to my cheek.

There were many times on nights previously that I had been hit with soft drinks, beer bottles, or even rocks when I used to work in outdoor venues. I have been cut from eye to cheek more than once by projectiles, and I found that shielding my face in this manner offered me a little protection. Vipe, being the monster that he was, liked to go around the ring a few times, scaring any old ladies or children that he could, tearing up an occasional guardrail and throwing it sideways from time to time. While that was going on, I made my way up the steps and through the ropes to get the microphone from the ring announcer. It was my turn to make a scene. I needed to make sure that the whole crowd hated me, hated us. In the business, we called that "getting heat."

"I was gonna come out here and tell you all what i really think of this town" I started, "but to be honest, I don't even remember the name of this dump." The boo's felt like a cool drink of water on a hot day.

"For God's sake, this state's motto should be, Louisiana: our women look like men."

Just then, a full tub of popcorn came from about the third row back. I quickly stepped back as it landed just in front of me at my feet. The Viper had come into the ring at this point and came to stand next to me. He bent over and began eating the popcorn off the canvas floor.

"For all you ladies in the audience that have ALL of your chromosomes, that's right, all three of you, i'd like for you to look at what a real man looks like."
I stepped back and let Viper flex and strut, the whole time chewing and throwing popcorn back into the crowd.

Our opponent was a local kid named Jerry Dindey. When I tell you that this guy was cheered on, it is an understatement. The people roared, I expected to see them toss babies in the air. Hell, I think he stopped and kissed a few on the way to the ring. He jumped in through the ropes and gave the stands a little wave, turning his back to Viper just as the bell rang. That was perfect. Vipe ran full speed over to him and clocked in the back of his head with his forearm. Again the crowd booed, wanting an immediate disqualification, but the beating only continued. Somewhere around the four minute mark, Jerry began to fight back. He threw a quick punch to Vipers midsection and the hulking figure winced slightly. The crowd began to rumble. He threw another quick jab, it connected and the crowd cheered again. The hero rose slowly to his feet, putting both hands on opposite sides of Vipers head. In one burst of energy, he leapt up and smashed his own head into the masked face of his opponent. The bigger of the two men staggered and the crowd favorite began to walk in circles around the ring, signaling to the people that it was time for the knockout blow.

Let me say something while it's in my head. When I say that Jerry was going to use his knockout blow, I mean he was literally going to end the match with a solid, jumping punch to his opponent's head. That was his finishing maneuver. Finishers were simpler back then, we protected them by making sure they were truly the ends of matches and the fans got used to that pattern and began to anticipate them. Slowly, over the years, finishers began to get more and more complex, and more and more dangerous. There was a time when smashing a guy head first to the mat put him in the hospital and out of action for months. I saw some yahoo in the

Philippines last year actually light himself on fire and jump off the top rope. Guess what? That wasn't even the finish. How in the hell are you supposed to continue wrestling after you've lit yourself on fire. Anyway, back to Jerry and Viper.

Jerry was standing with his fist up high, Viper was on one knww, the referee was checking to see if he was okay. While the official's back was turned I jumped up onto the ring apron, unbeknownst to the babyface. I raised up my cane, making sure to turn it flat, ensuring that poor Jerry wouldn't get seriously hurt, and cracked him right across the back. He fell like a sack of shit. As Jerry fell, Viper crawled immediately over and laid over the boy. The ref, not seeing what had occurred, dropped to his knees and counted the fall. The match was over. This may sound simple, but that's how easy it was back then to start a riot.

The chorus of jeers and the storm of flying debris started as soon as the officials hand hit the count of three. I went into the ring and stood next to Viper, holding his hand high in victory. That's when the real fun started. A fan climbed over the barricade and jumped between the ropes. Viper had his back turned to him so that left it up to me to handle it. I know that most people, when they meet me or see me, they see a spindly young kid with sort of a belly, glasses, and a loud mouth that needs to be shut. Truth is that they think I'm kind of soft. When it came to times like these though, trust me, i just didnt give a fuck.

This guy, fat as he was, came at us with quite a bit of speed. I stepped back onto my right foot and raised my cane back, making sure that this time, I turned that thing sideways. I came down right between this bastard's eyes. I fileted this guy. I mean, by the time I hit him, he was already bleeding from his shoes. Normally, you might think that would be the end of it, but no, that was just the beginning. Once that sliced up catfish hit the mat, the rest of the school started coming. Wave after wave of them spilled over and through the ropes, and I just kept swinging. Viper began to throw some of them back, too, creating a slight patch for us to get the hell out of there. This brings me to a big problem I have always had with the Mid-South area. The cops were too damn slow. Now this is probably because they were fans also, and they probably just got as mad at me as the kids in the front row, but for God's sake man, serve and protect.

Finally the boys in blue came around us and we began to make our way back up the aisle. Viper was out in front, I was right behind him and the cops were directly behind me. It was like one of those war formations from Sparta. We were only maybe three or four steps from the curtain when I saw a flash of light blue, and felt a sharp pain in my side. The flash was one of those old ladies with the cotton candy hair, and the pain was a stab wound. That old bitched knifed me. The cops grabbed her, and the other wrestlers who were watching dragged me through the curtain and into the locker room. THey sat me on a table and called for a doctor. In those parts, the term "doctor" was given away rather freely. This frail, decrepit man came to look at me. He poked and prodded at the hole in my side rather carelessly. I winced several times, the last one contained one of my usually colorful words. The old man shot me a look through his thick lenses.

"Oh. Does that hurt?"

"Yes motherfucker. It fucking hurts."

"Well maybe next time you won't get everyone all riled up."

I had so much heat that even though I was technically this guy's patient, he was trying to get revenge on me for costing the local boy his match. That's how it was back then. Viper sat next to me while this terrible doctor sewed me up and lectured us on right and wrong. I stuck a ci garette between my lips and Vipe was nice enough to light for me as I was having trouble moving my arm. I took a long deep drag and leaned my head back. Tomorrow was going to be another day and another town. It would be another building and another crowd, and I was going to have to do this all over again.

The Stool

There's something about woodworking. I don't know
if it's the feel or the simplicity, but I do know what I love the
most, the smell. The smell of fresh cut wood on a workbench
is just about the best damn thing in the world. That
unmistakable scent can raise the spirits and calm the nerves. It
can close distances and make houses feel like homes. I often
find myself, steaming coffee in hand, walking into my shop,
that beautiful aroma filling my nostrils thinking,
        "Can it get any better than this?"
And my wife says I don't appreciate the little things. Today
that smell welcomes me again, as I cross the threshold of my
garage.
        Sometimes I know what I'm making before picking
out the type of wood to use, other times, like today, I choose

the material first, and let that choice tell me what the project will be. Today I think a few boards of walnut will be my canvas. The dark surface and dark grain always makes for good, sturdy furniture. Something made from walnut is meant to have its strength tested, time and time again, supporting weight for years to come. Walnut, though, lacks the complexity of its cousins such as oak or mahogany, and should be crafted into a simple thing. I'm going to build a simple thing that is used and tested often. I am going to make a stool, perfect for a kitchen counter or a bar top, although I should probably avoid the latter.

I can't imagine what it was like in the old days, doing everything by hand. Now, all I have to do is flip a switch and feed the rough cut boards through a machine a few times and it spits out a perfectly flat plank. Planing used to be back-breaking work. Hour after hour, pushing and pulling, pushing and pulling, until the board is ready to be used. Thank goodness for the advancements made in modern woodworking.

I lay the chocolate color boards on my table and sit upon a stool, a stool I had built on a day much like today. I raise my coffee to my lips and only when I go to put it back down do I notice the tremor. I whip my arm back and forth to make it stop. My hands never used to shake before I went away, only when I came back. My wife knows this. She knows what I've seen. There's just some nights when I wonder if she understands. She says she does of course, but I know there are times when I see it in her eyes that she thinks I am crazy, and I believe I am not.

I rip the newly squared boards into ten, two inch strips and once again, put them out on the table. I stare at them, I stare as they lay there, trying to answer the question. The question is always the height. How high does one make a stool? Bar top? Kitchen?

"No, no," I whisper, "Those bases are all covered already."

There is also no need for anything to pull up to a desk , seats for those have already been made. Then it hits me. There is a large, dark, old barrel in the corner of our living room right next to our fireplace that we sometimes use as a snack table when we have guests. This will look perfect right beside it.

Cutting the legs and braces are easy on my miter saw. I remember when I was growing up I called it a chop saw, referring to the chopping motion it used to cut rip through timber. Four pieces at twenty four and a half inches, four pieces at thirteen and a half inches and four pieces at eight and a half inches. It's getting too easy. In the past, when I was away, it was always the moment when things felt easy that became the moment when the ground shook, and we were fearing for our lives. There's that goddamn wiggle in my hand again. I knew it was getting too easy.

I put the legs and braces aside for a moment and turn my attention to the seat. I cut eight pieces, all equal in size and plane, and sand them smooth. There are varying options on how to properly form them together but I always use the same method. I reach for my bottle of wood glue and place it on the table in front of me. I run a bead of the off white paste down the side of each of the pieces and push them together. I go over to my wall and select a few clamps which I have hanging there on an old piece of two by four I nailed up several years ago. A clamp is a craftsman's unsung hero amongst his tools. It may never be the first thing you think of when a wood shop comes to mind, but a good clamp is truly invaluable. I painstakingly and carefully poke and prod the eight pieces until they are level and square, then place three clamps on them, one in the middle and two on the ends.

This process takes me longer than it sounds. I am what you might call a stickler when it comes to details. I mean, I had to be. When you did what I did, were in charge like I was, you have to pay attention to the little things. That's why I get so damned mad when someone ignores them. I have seen first hand what can happen when the little things fall by the wayside and are overlooked. It's in me and I just don't want those things to be thought about. I want them to matter. Is that so much to ask?

"Why can't she get that?" I mutter to myself, waiting for the glue to dry.

Again I feel my hand begin to quake. I hold it up to my face and slowly start to touch the tip of my thumb to each of the hand's fingers. I repeat this over and over again until my hand stops trembling. In truth, it's been happening more and more now when I get angry or flustered. She's told the doctors that. I need to work on my temper, they say. That's why I come out here. The work calms me. My hand is usually still when I'm in my shop and free from my past, and my thoughts. Away from my memories of what I did. What I've done. What I might still do. There's that damn tremor again.

It's getting late and normally I'd quit for the day right about now, but I need to get this done. How amazing my wife's smile is when I give her one of my hand made pieces. All words and meaningless mistakes melt away, and there;s her smile. It's like we are kids again, long before I raised my steady right hand all those years ago. I look at that hand now, battered and bruised, not totally sure how or from what.

I distract myself by trying to decide on the jointery. There are so many options. I've used biscuit joints before, but don't know where my biscuit jointer is at the moment. There are several occasions I've used dowles or butt joints too. A company called Kregg came out with a wonderful jig that holds a piece of wood in place that makes perfect pocket holes. I see the red case that contains my dovetailing machine as well. There's a part of me that wants to pull out and tune up the old band saw and put in the work for a mortise and tenon, the strongest joint that can always takes the most time,

"She deserves that."

AS i make a move for my coffee, my shimmering hand misses the handle, and the mug goes crashing to the floor. The sound it makes seems to echo in my brain, reverberating off the walls of my skull in a constant, circular motion. That's when I feel it. I'm in a panic, alone. I begin to breathe heavily, the pattern of my chest becomes less and less orderly. I'm afraid. I ball my right hand into a fist, and the fear turns into something else. It becomes rage. I never used to be like this. I wasn't always afraid of noise. Now the littlest thing, a bang, a thud, a yell, makes me afraid. The fear is where the anger comes from. It causes me to do things I shouldn't. That is why I'm out here. It's all because of what I've done. I come out here and make something for her. A stool. I've made too many stools.

A Vegas Funeral

It's always hard being the new boyfriend. Especially
when you go to some kind of memorial service for one of her
friends just three weeks into the relationship. I took my seat in
the third row to the far left of the stage and waited in silence.
Yes, you heard me correctly, there was a stage. The memorial
service was in a showroom, a showroom that I had been in a
few times before, and a showroom that in a few weeks, I
would be working in. Before you start asking too many
questions, rest easy knowing that the body was not on the
stage or in the building. It was a service meant to celebrate the
life of a man, or at least I thought that's why we were there.
   I guess I should tell you that I am an entertainer. I
know that's the proper term to describe myself as I have now
met most everyone who uses other adjectives to paint a
picture of themselves and no, I'm not an actor, nor a musician,
not even a performer, I am an entertainer. I grew up in New
York, idolizing the greats, riding the subways and trains like

they did in the old days to get from gig to gig. I tried everything, improv, standup, music, jazz, burlesque, anything that was available to me. I did it all, not because I wanted the skills, or because I wanted to brag, but because I enjoyed everything, and yes, it seemed, in terms of audience reaction, that I was good at it.

I moved to Las Vegas in the winter, which is a hell of a time to drive across the country. The random storms and freezing temperatures of the midwest and the treachery of the mountains kept you on your toes through the long hours of travel. Along the way I was able to have my share of fun, hitting a few stages in random towns, testing myself to see how much appeal I really had. I found out on those cold nights that if the audience ain't buying what you're selling, you better change that tune real quick. That's what matters in the end, the audience. It's not about your artistic integrity, or your subjective view of what you're doing. If you are standing in front of a crowd, and the audience hates what they're seeing and hearing, you're bad. Case closed. They're not going to go home and talk about how great your character arc was, they'll remember if you make them laugh, or make them cry, nothing in between.

Roanoke, Virginia was quite the town. I found that I was far enough south that my thick, new york accent made whatever I was saying funny to them. It almost felt like cheating. They were nice people and the beer was cheap. The bar I ended up staying in had the grille of a 57 Chevy sticking right out of the wall. The taps were coming right out of the radiator. The bartender had a southern accent and blue eyes. If it wasn't for Nashville I'd say it was the best stop on my journey. I got onto a stage in the heart of Tennessee. There was a fiddle player with long legs and a pretty smile. I'm such a sucker for musicians. Her name was Ali, and I'll never forget her. The guy that brought me up was this old, rum runner looking dude with a long beard and skinny hands. They brought me up and I sang Wagon Wheel. It was the sixth time that song had been done that night, but no one seemed to care.

Vegas was different in a lot of ways from New York. First off there were plenty of shows for all different types of entertainers. It didn't matter if you were a singer or a comic or an actor, there was an opportunity for you there. That doesn't mean that you didn't need another job to get by. But, hey, if you really love what you're doing you'll tend a cash register a couple days a week to make more money, right? The comedy scene was probably the biggest difference I saw when I moved. At home, you would go into a real club where there would be real people there to listen to your jokes. In Vegas I was standing in the corner of a room, talking to myself while the other "comedians," smoked cigarettes outside and a few guys at the bar played keno for twenty bucks at a time.

The biggest thing I noticed about Vegas were the egos. Now I'm not saying that New York didn't have egos, of course it did. I as an entertainer myself have an ego, which has grown over the years as I have put in my time and mileage honing my craft and skill set. In Vegas I met people who would come to me with the bravado and panache of a true stage veteran, only to head up and lay the largest goose egg that's ever been seen on this earth. Then they'd come down and talk of triumph and success, while my mouth hung open in shock and awe at the lack of self awareness. Where I'm from, an ego is something that is grown, and those who don't have the skill to match are always taken down a peg by the more seasoned performers. I never walked up to anyone in a club and complained about why I wasn't getting booked. If I wasn't being put on shows, I simply must not have been good enough, so I worked harder until I was.

Anyway, I'm losing my place, I'm sorry. It took a few weeks for me to start getting consistent bookings on local shows but it happened. Most of those were as a standup, so that's what I became known as in the town. I was doing what is known as opening for someone at a small bar off the strip one night, when the booker told me that he was going to let this girl do a guest spot to start the show, which is only about five minutes before the two main comics go on. This is the girl I would end up going to the memorial service with, or rather, for. Now as this is a story about a specific moment of my life and not a general overview of it, I'm not going to get into details about how I felt watching this girl or what she looked like. All that needs to be known that is relevant to this tale, is that I was smitten and I began to date her.

She was in a show on the strip, in one of the older and more dingy casinos that had a ton of history to it. I went to see the show a few times as it was a dinner show and I can never say no to a free meal. After one of the performances the casting director came up to me and questioned my background and experience. I had no idea they were looking for a new cast member, but there I was being auditioned out of nowhere. I was told within minutes that I would be getting contacted by the assistant director that week to schedule an afternoon to come to the showroom for a walkthrough and rehearsal. I was over the moon. I remember walking through the casino holding her hand, feeling nothing beneath my feet, smiling from ear to ear. As we hopped onto the escalator to the parking garage, she introduced me to an older man standing in front of us as one of her oldest friends. He was a tall, distinguished looking fellow, a real gentleman type. His thick gray hair eased backward, his face was freshly shaven, and his eyes were like dabs of chocolate, filled with the kind of knowledge that can only be gotten from living life. He wore a jet black sweater with a golden zipper that only went about halfway up his torso and bowed his head at making my acquaintance. His name was Dominic.

About a week later, as foretold, I received an email from the assistant director of the show telling me he would like to meet on the 11th for the rehearsal and walkthrough. I hurriedly responded as I couldn't believe that I was actually going to be in a real Las Vegas show. A few minutes later my phone rang. It was her. I picked up, thinking she had heard about my scheduled rehearsal and wanted to congratulate me. All I heard on the other end of the phone were sobs. I tried to get her to calm down and tell me what happened. After a few moments she was able to calm herself long enough to tell me that Dominic was dead. He had been on his daily jog when he'd had a heart attack. She told me that he was an avid workout fanatic and did everything the doctor told him to, including having a glass and a half of red wine a day. I learned later that heart disease ran in his family. I guess we can't outrun our genetics.

It was Dominic's memorial service that I was now attending. I wore all black with a touch of red as one should for such an occasion. I hate funerals. I guess that's not really much of a surprise. I mean who actually likes them? The sheer amount of raw emotion at a funeral is always overwhelming.

Anyone that has ever been to a wake or sat shiva, knows the eerie feeling that comes over someone when they enter a place where mourning is taking place. Sitting is a room watching the faces of every person that walked through the door, looking at the closest of kin sitting up front where everyone can see them, when all they really want to do is be alone in their grief. I always thought that was just added torture. My loved one is dead, so let me be forced to say hello to everyone and make small talk while I ignore this freshly made hole in my heart. Then there is always one person from the family who was talked into speaking. Trying to give some sort of eulogy through a red face and tears. The whole experience is always just gut wrenching whether you're there for support or necessity. Man how I wish this memorial was like one of those.

The room was filled with people who considered themselves close to Dominic. Former castmates, casting directors, producers, sound technicians. Oddly enough there was only one person I met that was actually a family member. His poor wife. She sat in the middle of the theater clutching to a tissue, here eyes pink from no doubt a week of irritation. The casting director spoke first. She was a real piece of work. One of the types of people who has dinner in the same restaurant as a celebrity once and then brags about it for the rest of their life. Being the casting director of a dinner show in Las Vegas is basically as prestigious as being a hiring manager at a Wendy's. The bottom line being, it's just a job. As I watched her hard faced expression spitting out meaningless words, I realized another reason she was in the position she was in. She was a bad actor. I don't mean that she wasn't really upset about the passing of Dominic, she was.

I'm just saying she was trying really hard to look upset, and she was failing at it.

When she finally finished her scene, I was relieved. She let everyone know that anyone was able to come up and speak if they wanted to. I was shocked at the amount of people who stood up to go up on stage. Who volunteers to speak at a funeral? If you're specifically asked to do so, I get that, but volunteer? The parade of bodies that went up on stage was never ending. Each one telling a, no doubt true story, about them and Dominic. Trying desperately to convey just how much his passing had affected them. I sat, flabbergasted as no one talked of his family or his wife, just themselves. It hit me that this had become a competition, a contest. The idea was to see who was the most upset, the most affected by this tragedy. It wasn't a service to celebrate a man's life. It was a chance for a few low level performers to lap up some stage time, and get a round of applause. People even sang songs. Again, who sings at a funeral?

As I look back at it, the few people that didn't speak were the only people whom, after getting to know them for the few years I did the show, were the only ones I came out of my time there with great respect for. The assistant director, a real stand up guy. Someone who takes their job just the right amount of serious, but also has plenty of self awareness and knows that there are more important things in life than dinner theater. He was probably the one true friend I made from that experience, and I enjoy that friendship to this day. He'd known Dominic a long time and he didn't speak. He knew better. He's a real person.

As the charade came to a close, Dominc's wife got up to speak. That poor woman. She spoke kind, loving words about her husband, and thanked everyone for being there. Her closing line assured everyone that she knew she had a difficult road ahead, and that she would navigate it the best she could because she knew she had the support of the people in the room. That's when my heart broke. I knew that when the lights faded, when the stage was gone and there was no performance to give, these people wouldn't be there for her. They'd be wherever they could find the light, wherever they could hear the crowd, and that sure wasn't in her living room.

Not surprisingly, that show closed. With such a collection of self important hacks in charge, how could it not? It did reopen a few years later, only to close again. They had let the same inmates run the old asylum again. They'll never learn. Truth be told I always enjoyed doing it, the show. I got to make people laugh and collect a paycheck for it. Problem was there were too many cooks in the kitchen, too many opinions of what the show was or what it should be. There weren't enough people just grateful to be there. There were so many individuals that I met in Vegas that felt that being a professional entertainer was entitled, a god given right by birth. In reality anyone that can make a living at going on a stage is lucky, they're privileged. The act of making a real living doing what you truly love is special. I don't think enough people get that. I still perform sometimes, but much less than I once did. I've come to hate most of the personalities it forces me to interact with. I much prefer sitting here, writing my thoughts. This way I don't have to deal with all the egos, only mine.

The Provider : Door-To-Door

Today, the world of door-to-door sales is virtually nonexistent. Sure, you might get some weirdos on your porch asking you about solar energy or questioning your faith and salvation, but none of which are carrying and selling the actual, tangible product. No one does what I used to do, which was walk the streets, knocking on doors, holding a large leather case in one hand and a few brochures in the other, selling everyday items to everyday folks. The best part was, these were things that would generally improve their lives. Most people ask me,

"How did you know you would be good at sales?" And to be honest, I have no earthly idea that I'd be any good at it. I was out around town with a few guys, having a few laughs, and they got to telling me that they thought I'd make a great salesman. Now, I had no idea if these guys had any idea what they were talking about, but I needed a job. That was that. That's how I got my first job in sales working for The Fuller Brush Company.

The Fuller Brush Company was founded way back in 1906 by Alfred Fuller in the basement shop of his house in Somerville, Massachusetts. When I worked for Fuller I was a door-to-door salesman in the southern region of Ohio selling brushes and combs of various sorts, including hair brushes that had a lifetime's guarantee for which we became kind of famous. Currently, when I talk about door-to-door sales, people tend to wonder how it could be enjoyable or even profitable. I do want to remind these people that we didn't live or operate in your high tech world of home security systems with your fancy doorbell cameras that alert you when a mouse crawls across your garbage can at three in the morning. It was a different time, a time where if there was a knock at the door, there was a feeling of genuine excitement over who that visitor might be and the possible joy they might bring to an otherwise humdrum day.

Once I started, I learned pretty quickly that although people would answer their door, it didn't mean they would always be happy to see you. They would just as soon shut the door in your face once they realized you werent their neighbor coming over for an afternoon cocktail or Grandma visiting to see the kids, and also have a cocktail. I got it in my head early, that if I were to have any chance at making a living with this thing, I had to stop those doors from being slammed in my face. How did I do this? I actually made it impossible for the homeowner to close the door physically. I know it sounds weird, let me explain. As I stepped onto the porch or stoop of a home, I would turn sideways, pressing my heavy, leather case against the closed door. Then, I would knock. When the homeowner answered the door, I would turn to face them making sure my case swung into the doorway. I would then place the case down, freeing my hand to fish out a brochure from my inside jacket pocket. With the case being placed across the doors threshold, being half outside and half in the house, it made it impossible for the door to be completely shut because my case would hold it open. I realize now that this does sound a little aggressive, but it gave me the precious few seconds I needed to crack a line and get a smile. Once I got them to smile, an invitation into their home usually followed. It was then that I was able to sit down and get into my sales presentation.

This is where you really needed to be dialed in. It didn't matter how many houses you got into, if your presentation was shit, you made no money. I modeled mine much like I would my magic act. It had an opener, middle, and closer. All of the spots were specifically designed to display the strength and durability of the brushes and combs sold by Fuller. My favorite part of my presentation was always the grand finale. I learned way back when, as I was doing my act in the back of an old theater, you want to leave your best trick for last, this way you leave your audience in a true state of shock and awe. They always remember what you do last rather than what you did first. The keynote for me, was to take one of Fuller's patented combs, grip it in both hands, and viciously bend that son of a bitch in half. I was in hundreds of homes and always ended it this way. That thing never broke, never. Although, there was one time I did get a little scare.

Winters in the Midwest are cold. They're really cold. This is both good and bad for door-to-door sales. Obviously, it's bad because you're walking the streets, in the snow and sleet, carrying that goddamn bag trying not to catch your death. On the other hand, it's good because people are more likely to take pity and invite you out of the cold and into their home to at least warm yourself for a few moments, and like I said before, a few moments was all I needed. On this particular night, I had been invited out of the harsh weather and found myself presenting to a family. It was going wonderfully. The time came for my big finish. I took out that comb and gripped it with two hands. I looked over to the kids and gave them a little wink. They giggled. It's always good to let kids think you're letting them in on something that their parents dont know. It gets them on your side, and if you got the kids, it makes the sale all the more easier. As I bent the comb in half, my heart stopped. To both my shock and horror, I heard a loud and obnoxious crack.

Like I said, Ohio winters are brutally cold. There wasn't much insulation in that display case I carried. Each item in that case however, was wrapped in a sleeve of wax paper. The bitter temperatures froze this wax paper and it crinkled and cracked in my hands. The Fuller comb had passed its test yet again and from that moment on, whenever I sat down in a home, I made sure to place my case near a heater or a fire to ensure that little snafu never happened again. My job was hard enough without that shit happening again.

There comes a time in any salesman's life, when he has to move onto bigger and better things. For Me that ended up being both literal and figurative. I left the world of brushes and combs to pettle every salesman's dream. As crazy as this may sound to some, I was employed by The Singer Company as a door-to-door salesman. Yes, that's right, I sold sewing machines door-to-door. It was not only bigger and better, but also heavier. Just like with Fuller Brush though, I knew I had a damn good product. Honestly, I think that is the real secret to sales. If I learned anything about actually selling, it is that when you truly believe in what you are trying to give to people, that makes the sale all the more easy. It's like you're not really selling a product, you're selling your belief.

Pettling something new meant creating a new presentation. The Singer sewing machine was by far the best manually powered sewing machine on the market. Its clean and simple design allowed for maximum precision and performance. I decided to showcase its abilities by sewing through different materials, all of various thickness and weight. I would start off with a standard swatch of cotton, then move onto some canvas, then perhaps a piece of heavy denim and so on and so forth. With Singer, just as I had with Fuller, I came up with a real mind blowing final demonstration. All the previous swatches had been of material that would commonly be placed in a sewing machine. I decided to sew through something that no one would ever think to sew. When the time came, I would routinely reach into my bag just as I had done several times before, and produce, not a swath of fabric, but a cut piece of a wooden yard stick.

This act alone always prompted a variety of reactions from whoever I was in front of. The husband would usually snicker, the wife's eyes would open in amazement, and the kids would always giggle, which would lead me to give them a wink, again letting them in on a joke that their parents were not in on. There were several times that I would even take wagers or poll the families to see who thought my machine was up to the task. Often I would joke that the yard stick was no thicker than a pair of dad's old underwear, which always got the kids on my side. When all the lines were cracked, and I had everyone thoroughly entertained, it was time to get on with it. I would hold the stick out in front of everyone, showcasing it like I would a playing card plucked from a deck, I'd then place it right up against the needle. My sleeves would be rolled up, followed by an exaggerated cracking of my knuckles and finally a deep breath. It was like I was a circus performer getting ready to place my head in the lion's mouth. As the mood was set, I would place my foot upon the iron pedal, and get that needle going, and sew right though the piece of wood, no problem. I'd then snip it free from the threaded needle and hold it out for each family member to see. It was just the prestige at the end of any good magic trick. Only this wasn't any type of illusion, it was just an amazing piece of machinery performing at the level it was designed to do. After that, there was usually nothing left to do but fill out their order form, write them their receipt, and continue on my way. I truly loved selling those things, but all good things must come to an end.

The Singer Company had been founded in 1851 by I.M. Singer and Co. It eventually became The Singer Manufacturing COmpany, which was the name that I worked under. What eventually happened, believe it or not, was that the company decided that the machines that they were manufacturing, the machines that myself and others were making a very nice living selling, were actually too good. As dumb as that sounds, heres how it was actually explained to me. Year after year the machines that had been purchased worked as they always had, never needing anything more than routine maintenance and upkeep. The brainiacs in the financial division of the company had decided that this income based only on minor repairs and fixes, could not alone keep the company afloat. They wanted to move on to selling brand new electric sewing machines, only the old ones were far better pieces of machinery. Upon hearing this, I decided to leave the company, rather than try to sell a clearly inferior product. On my last day at SInger, I was leaving the plant and saw something that I have never and will never forget. There were several large men tossing brand new sewing machines into dumpsters, and several, larger men, smashing those machines to pieces. Progress, they said. I never understood that. Still dont. I never will.

The Game

The score was two to one, the home team was behind.
There was just one out left for our boys in our last at bat.
Hodges dug in, his high blue stirrups caked in dirt from a long
afternoon. It had been a long summer for him, but this was a
chance to make us all forget about that. He wagged his bat,
back and forth, back and forth, as if he was trying to find
something, and then, like he'd suddenly found it, the bat
landed gently on his shoulder. Yes, our Gillie boy was ready.

On the mound was the Dandy, who'd had our number
all day. The crowd had that familiar hum in anticipation, as he
spun into his windup. The ball audibly cut through the air and
landed with a loud crack in the catcher's mitt,

"Strike one," called the umpire.
A chorus of boo's and hisses filled the air, the shrill noise
lasting longer than the time between pitches as the Dandy
coiled and fired again. Hodges took his stride, but the bat
remained on his shoulder,

"Strike two."

This time there were no boo's, only the sound of the faithful quietly accepting what was next to come. They all gathered their belongings, ready to head home. It's not that they wanted to go, only that they knew the chances, like I said, we'd seen this all summer. I, myself, knowing full well I had an article due the next morning, slid my pen into my notebook and furied it away, deep in my pocket. The pitcher got his sign and once more drew into his motion. Gil's bat never moved from its perch upon his shoulder, it stayed true as he watched the ball in the dirt; ball one. Another pitch, another ball, two and two. Still no one paid much attention as the ball was thrown again; ball three. The crowd this time stayed silent, but together they halted their march to the exits. I inched myself up in my chair, placing my hands beneath my chin, staring at the mound.

The Dandy was standing awkwardly, his cap in his hand, his arm wiping his brow. He was sweating. The mighty ace who had stifled us all day, was sweating. This type of nervous display I hadn't seen much of. Quietly I sat, watching as the pitcher placed his hat back upon his head and began to feverishly rub the ball, as if he was searching for answers. There was something else too. His eyes were no longer focused on his battery mate, nor were they fixed on the hitter, instead they were darting around the ball park, the stands, the field, everywhere they shouldn't have been. In the batters box, Gillie was only focused on the pitcher, his feet never shifting, the bat never leaving his shoulder. It was pretty clear that our Gillie boy was ready.

As the hurler returned to the rubber, I reached into my pocket and retrieved my pad and pen. This was going to be the day it all turned around. The catcher flashed a sign that was the affreement of the Dandy and the lanky right hander rocked and fired. The blazing fastball was met with a strong swing by the waiting batter and was promptly fouled straight back behind home plate. A collective gasp momentarily sucked the air from the ballpark. As the ball was retrieved, the crowd now began to rise in unison. The faithful applause was not quite as loud as it had been in the past. There was still very much a feeling of dread in the air. The pitcher rubbed and wiped the ball again, still showing his nerves. Hodges swung his bat in furious circles, his confidence growing with each completed loop. Once again, the backstop gave the sign and once again, the Dandy nodded with approval. His set was a bit longer this time, perhaps trying to throw off the timing of the hitter. The baseball hissed in, and was met with a swing from our Gillie boy. The foul this time shot straight back, harder than it was thrown and the crowd again drew in its breath. That scene repeated itself twice more fully, whipping the crowd into a frenzy.

There are certain moments in sports that someone in my profession never forgets. I can tell you as you read this, that the battle myself and anyone else at Ebbet's this day was witnessing one of these moments.

The Giants' manager had seen though. He waddled his way out to the mound to have a talk with his struggling ace. The veteran leader could see his prize rose wilting in the hot brooklyn sun. As the conference took place Gillie stepped out of the batter's box, bent at the waist and scooped up a bit of dirt which he rubbed deep into his hands. I glazed down to the visitors bullpen but saw that there were no arms being loosened by the opposing club. The Dandy was to finish this one on his own. The meeting concluded with a hearty pat on the butt as the slipper walked slowly back to his dugout, both hands buried deep in his back pockets.

The pitcher stood behind the rubber, breathing heavily, pounding the ball into his glove repeatedly beneath his chin. Finally, seemingly ready for the moment, he toes the block peering in for the sign. Hodges took his place back in the box, making his familiar circles with his bat. All seemed to be set as the Dandy swung his arms over his head and came forward, unleashing one more sizzling fastball. Gillie uncoiled himself, whipping the bat through the zone and connecting with the pitch. The audible crack, echoing throughout the stands, brought us all to our feet.

We all watched as the high fly ball sailed deep out into the left center field. Fillie ran hard down to first back, his head up, watching the flight path of the ball. The Dandy starred out, his hands on his knees, clearly dismayed by what was happening. Down on the third base line, the manager of our boys leaned himself back, as if his will would affect the distance. The sphere itself reached its maximum height and began to make its way back down to earth. I could see the patrons in the bleachers reaching out to catch it. After what seemed like years, the ball finally landed deep into....

... the glove of the centerfielder.

I sank back into my seat, a crushed notepad in my hand. The Brooklyn faithful quietly began to go home and back to their lives. It was as if the whole city had fallen silent. That, of course, was not true as the cries of children and sobs of adults were easily heard leaving the ballpark. I looked back out to the field. Hodges was standing between first and second, the lone figure left on the massive diamond. He stayed still, his hands on his hips, his uniform covered in sweat and dirt. His blue number 15 hung high on his slumped shoulders as he looked out to where the ball had been caught. The stands were empty now, the fans were all gone, but they will be back. There are still more games to be played, more pitches to be thrown, and more at bats to be had . That will always be the beauty of the game. As for the loss today, none of us were really surprised. After all, we'd seen this all summer.

Made in the USA
Middletown, DE
13 February 2022

60902813R00057